THE
MAGIC
BED-KNOB

By the same author

MARY NORTON

THE MAGIC
BED-KNOB

Illustrated by
Anthony Lewis

DENT CHILDREN'S BOOKS
LONDON

This edition first published in 1993
Reprinted in 1998
First published in 1945
Text copyright © Mary Norton, 1945 and 1957
Illustrations copyright © Anthony Lewis, 1993

The right of Mary Norton and Anthony Lewis
to be identified as the Author and the Illustrator of this work
has been asserted by them in accordance with the Copyright,
Designs and Patents Act 1988.

Typeset by Deltatype Ltd, Ellesmere Port
Printed in Great Britain
for J. M. Dent by
Butler & Tanner Ltd, Frome and London
The Orion Publishing Group
Orion House
5 Upper St Martin's Lane
London WC2H 9EA

A catalogue record for this book is available from the British Library

For
Robin and Chick

Contents

Once upon a time there were three children and their names were Carey, Charles, and Paul. Carey was about your age, Charles a little younger, and Paul was only six.

One summer they were sent to Bedfordshire to stay with an aunt. She was an old aunt and she lived in an old square house – which lay in a garden where no flowers grew. There were lawns and shrubs and cedars but no flowers, which made the garden seem grave and sad.

The children were shy of the house, with its big hall and wide stairways; they were shy of Elizabeth – the stern old housemaid – and they were shy of their aunt, too, because she had pale blue eyes with pinkish edges and did not often smile. But they loved the garden and river which ran through it and the countryside beyond with its tangled hedges and sweet meadow grass.

They were out all day.

They played in the barns, they played by the river, and

they played in the lanes and on the hills. They were punctual for meals because they were visitors and good children at heart. One day slipped into another and all the days were alike – until Miss Price hurt her ankle. And that's where the story begins.

You all know somebody rather like Miss Price. She wore grey coats and skirts and had a long thin neck with a scarf round it made of Liberty silk with a Paisley pattern. Her nose was sharply pointed and she had very clean, pink hands. She rode on a high bicycle with a basket in front, and she visited the sick and taught the piano. She lived in a neat little house which stood in a lane at the bottom of the garden and the children knew her by sight and always said 'Good morning.' In all the village there was none so ladylike as Miss Price.

Now, one day, the children decided to go mushroom picking before breakfast. They awoke almost before the night had drained away from the sleeping house and tiptoed through the hall in their stockinged feet. When they got outside the garden was very still and drenched in dew, and, as they walked, their shoes left black smudges in the pearly grass. They spoke in whispers because it seemed as if the world, except the birds, were still asleep.

Suddenly, Paul stood still, staring down the slope of the lawn towards the darkness of the cedars. 'What's that?'

They all stopped and they all stared.

'It moved,' Paul told them. 'Come on, let's see.'

Carey sped ahead on her long legs. 'It's a person,' she called back and then her step grew slower. She waited until they caught up with her. 'It's –' her voice was hushed with surprise, 'it's Miss Price!'

And so it was, sitting there on the wet ground under the

cedar. Her grey coat and skirt was torn and crumpled and her hair hung down in wisps.

'Oh, poor Miss Price,' cried Carey, running up, 'whatever's the matter? Have you hurt yourself?'

Miss Price looked back with frightened eyes and then she looked away.

'It's my ankle,' she muttered.

Carey fell on her knees in the damp grass. Miss Price's ankle was indeed the strangest shape. 'Oh, poor Miss Price,' cried Carey again, and the tears came to her eyes. 'It must hurt terribly.'

'It does,' said Miss Price.

'Run to the house, Charles,' ordered Carey, 'and tell them to ring up the doctor.'

Then a strange look came over Miss Price's face and her eyes opened wide as if with fright. 'No, no,' she stammered, gripping Carey's arm. 'No, not that: just help me to get home.'

The children looked at her, but they were not surprised. It did not even occur to them to wonder what Miss Price might be doing so early in the morning in their aunt's garden.

'Help me to get home,' repeated Miss Price. 'I can put one arm round your shoulders –' She looked at Carey. 'And one round his. Then, perhaps, I can hop.'

Paul watched seriously as Carey and Charles leaned towards Miss Price. Then he sighed. 'And I'll carry this,' he said obligingly, picking up a garden broom.

'We don't want that,' Carey told him sharply. 'Put it up against the tree.'

'But it's Miss Price's.'

'How do you mean – Miss Price's? It's the garden broom.'

Paul looked indignant. 'It isn't ours. It's hers. It's what

she fell off. It's what she rides on.'

Carey and Charles stood up, their faces red from stooping, and stared at Paul.

'What she rides on?'

'Yes. Don't you, Miss Price?'

Miss Price became paler than ever. She looked from one child to another. She opened her mouth and then she shut it again, as if no words would come.

'You're quite good at it, aren't you, Miss Price?' Paul went on encouragingly. 'You weren't at first.'

Then Miss Price began to cry. She pulled out her handkerchief and held it over her face. 'Oh dear,' she said, 'oh, dear! Now I suppose everybody knows.'

Carey put her arms round Miss Price's neck. It was what you always did to people when they cried.

'It's all right, Miss Price. Nobody knows. Nobody knows at all. Paul didn't even tell us. It's quite all right. I think it's wonderful to ride on a broomstick.'

'It's very difficult,' said Miss Price, but she blew her nose.

They helped her to her feet. Carey felt puzzled and very excited, but she didn't like to ask any more. Slowly and painfully they made their way through the garden and down the lane that led to Miss Price's house. The rising sun glimmered through the hedgerows and turned the dust in the roadway to pale gold. Carey and Charles went very carefully, and Miss Price flapped between like a large, grey bird with a broken wing.

Paul walked behind – with the broomstick.

*A*fterwards, on the way home, Carey and Charles tackled Paul.

'Paul, why didn't you tell us you'd seen Miss Price on a broomstick?'

'I dunno.'

'But, Paul, you ought to have told us. We'd have liked to see it, too. It was very mean of you, Paul.'

Paul did not reply.

'When did you see her?'

'In the night.'

Paul looked stubborn. He felt as if he might be going to cry. Miss Price always passed so quickly. She would have been gone before he could call anyone and they would have said at once, 'Don't be silly, Paul.' Besides, it had been his secret, his nightly joy. His bed was beside the window and, when the moon was full, it shone on his pillow and wakened him. It had been exciting to lie there, with his eyes fixed on the pale sky beyond the ragged blackness of the cedar boughs. Some nights he did not wake up. Other nights he woke up and she did not come. But he saw her often enough and, each time he saw her, she had learned to fly a little better. At first she had wobbled so, balanced sideways on the stick, that he wondered why she did not ride astride. She would grip the broomstick with one hand and try to hold her hat on with the other, and her feet, in their long shoes, looked so odd against the moonlit sky. Once she fell – and the broomstick came down quite slowly, like an umbrella blown inside out, with Miss Price clinging to the handle. Paul had watched her anxiously until she reached the ground. That time she landed safely.

Partly, he did not tell because he wanted to be proud of Miss Price. He did not want the others to see her until she was really good at it; until, perhaps, she could do tricks on a broomstick and look confident instead of scared. Once when she had lifted both hands in the air at the same time, Paul nearly clapped. He knew that was hard to do even on a bicycle.

'You see, Paul,' Carey grumbled, 'it was really very selfish; now Miss Price has hurt her ankle, she won't be flying again for ages. Charles and I may never have the chance of seeing her!'

Later, as they were solemnly eating lunch in the high, dark dining-room, Aunt Beatrice startled them by saying suddenly, 'Poor Miss Price!' They all looked up, as if she had read their secret thoughts, and were relieved when she went on calmly: 'It seems she has fallen off her bicycle and sprained her ankle. So painful, poor soul. I must send her down some peaches.'

Paul sat with his spoon half-way to his mouth and his eyes moved round from Charles to Carey.

Carey cleared her throat. 'Aunt Beatrice,' she said, 'could we take the peaches to Miss Price?'

'That's very thoughtful of you, Carey. I don't see why not, if you know where she lives.'

Paul seemed about to burst into speech but was silenced by a kick from Charles; aggrievedly, he swallowed his last mouthful of rice pudding.

'Yes, Aunt Beatrice, we do know where she lives.'

It was about four o'clock in the afternoon when the children knocked at Miss Price's neat front door. The path on which they stood was gaily bordered with flowers and, through the half-open windows of the sitting-room, Miss Price's dimity curtains fluttered in the breeze. The door was opened by Agnes, a village girl who served Miss Price for a few hours daily.

As the children entered the little sitting-room, for a moment they felt very shy. There lay Miss Price on the sofa, her bandaged foot raised up on pillows. She still looked pale, but now her hair was tidy and her white blouse spotlessly neat.

'What lovely peaches! Thank you, my dears, and thank your aunt. Very kind of her, I'm sure. Sit down, sit down.'

The children sat down gingerly on the little spindly chairs.

'Agnes is making us some tea. You must stay and keep me company. Carey, can you open that card table?'

The children bustled round and helped to set the room for tea. A little table near Miss Price for the tea-tray and a white cloth on the card table for the scones, the bread and butter, the quince jelly, and the ginger cake.

They enjoyed their tea and, when it was over, they helped Agnes to clear away. Then Miss Price showed Charles and

Carey how to play backgammon and lent Paul a large book full of pictures called *Paradise Lost*. Paul liked the book very much. He liked the smell of it and the gilt-edged pages.

When they had finished the game of backgammon and it seemed that it must be nearly time to go home, Carey took her courage in both hands.

'Miss Price,' she said hesitatingly, 'if it isn't rude to ask – are you a witch?'

There was silence for a moment, and Carey could feel her heart beating. Paul looked up from his book.

Very carefully, Miss Price closed the backgammon board and laid it on the little table beside the sofa. She took up her knitting and unfolded it.

'Well,' she said slowly, 'I am and I'm not.'

Paul sat back on his heels. 'You mean, you are sort of,' he suggested.

Miss Price threw him a glance. 'I mean, Paul,' she said quietly, 'that I am studying to be a witch.' She knitted a few stitches, pursing up her mouth.

'Oh, Miss Price!' cried Carey warmly. 'How terribly clever of you!'

It was the best thing she could have said. Miss Price flushed but she looked pleased.

'How did you first think of it, Miss Price?'

'Well, ever since I was a girl, I've had a bit of a gift for witchcraft, but somehow – what with piano lessons and looking after my mother – I never seemed to have the time to take it up seriously.'

Paul was staring at Miss Price, as if to drink in every detail of her appearance. 'I don't think you're a wicked witch,' he said at last.

Miss Price dropped her eyes unhappily. 'I know, Paul,'

she admitted in a low voice. 'You're quite right. I started too late in life. That's the whole trouble.'

'Is being wicked the hardest part?' asked Carey.

'It is for me,' Miss Price told her rather sadly. 'But there are people who have a natural gift for it.'

'Paul has,' said Charles.

Paul came nearer and sat down on a chair. He was still staring at Miss Price, as if he longed to ask her something. After a minute, he found courage. 'Could you just do a little bit of magic for us now?'

'Oh, Paul,' exclaimed Carey, 'don't worry Miss Price: she can't do magic with a sprained ankle.'

'Yes, she could,' protested Paul hotly, 'she could do it lying down, couldn't you, Miss Price?'

'Well,' said Miss Price, 'I am a little tired, Paul. But I'll just do a little quick one and then you must all go home. There you are!'

Carey and Charles looked around quickly, following the direction of Miss Price's eyes. Paul's chair was empty. Paul had gone – but where he had been sitting perched a little yellow frog.

Before Carey or Charles had time to exclaim, Paul was back again, still staring expectantly at Miss Price.

'Oh,' cried Carey, with a gasp, 'that was wonderful, wonderful! How *did* you do it?'

She felt breathless and almost afraid, magic – a spell – she had seen it with her own eyes.

'I didn't see anything,' complained Paul.

Carey looked at him impatiently. 'Oh, don't be silly, Paul. You turned into a frog. You must have felt it.'

Paul's lips trembled. 'I didn't feel anything,' he said, in a squeaky little voice. But nobody heard him. Carey was

staring at Miss Price with shining eyes.

'Miss Price,' she pointed out almost reproachfully, 'you could have done that at the church concert, instead of singing.'

Miss Price laid down her knitting. A strange look crept into her face, and she looked hard at Carey as if she were seeing her for the first time. Nervously, Carey drew back in her chair.

'Although you sing so nicely,' she added quickly.

But Miss Price did not seem to hear. There was a wild light in her eyes and her lips moved quietly, as if she were reciting. 'There must be some way,' she was saying slowly. 'There – must – be – some – way . . .'

'Some way of what?' asked Charles, after a moment's uncomfortable silence.

Miss Price smiled, showing her long yellow teeth.

'Of keeping your mouths shut,' she rapped out.

Carey was shocked. This was far from ladylike. 'Oh, Miss Price!' she exclaimed unhappily.

'Of keeping your mouths shut,' repeated Miss Price slowly, smiling more unpleasantly than ever.

Paul made a little wriggling movement in his chair. 'Now she's getting wicked,' he whispered to Carey in a pleased voice.

Carey drew away from him as if she had not heard. She looked worried. 'What do you mean, Miss Price? You mean we mustn't tell anyone that –' She hesitated.

'That you're a witch?' put in Paul.

But Miss Price was still staring, as if she neither heard nor saw. 'In just a minute I'll think of something,' she said, as if to herself. 'In just a minute –'

Then Carey did something which Charles thought very

brave. She got up from her chair and sat down beside Miss Price on the sofa.

'Listen, Miss Price,' she said. 'We did try to help you when you hurt your ankle. There isn't any need to use any kind of nasty magic on us. If you want to stop us telling, you could do it in a nice kind of way.'

Miss Price looked at her. 'How could I do it in a nice kind of way?' she asked, but she sounded more reasonable.

'Well,' said Carey, 'you could give us something – something magic – and if we told anyone about you, we'd have to forfeit it. You know, like a game. Directly we told, the thing would stop being magic.'

'What sort of a thing?' asked Miss Price, but as if the idea held possibilities.

Charles leaned forward. 'Yes,' he put in, 'a ring or something that we could twist and a slave comes. And, if we told about you, the slave wouldn't come any more. Couldn't you do that?'

Miss Price looked thoughtful. 'I couldn't manage a slave,' she said after a moment.

'Well, something like that.'

Miss Price sat very quiet. She was thinking hard. 'I know,' she said, after a while. Suddenly, she seemed quite nice and cheerful again. 'There's something I've been wanting to try out. Mind you, I'm not sure that it will work. Has anybody got a ring on them?'

Alas, none of them had. Paul felt in his pockets, just in case, but found nothing but the brass knob he had unscrewed from his bed that morning.

'Well, anything. A bracelet would do. It should be something you can twist.'

But unfortunately Carey could not produce a bracelet

either. 'I have one at home,' she said, 'but I only wear it on Sundays.'

'You can twist this,' cried Paul suddenly, holding out the bed-knob. 'That's just what it does. It twists and it twists and it twists. I twisted it off,' he added rather unnecessarily.

Miss Price took the bed-knob and held it thoughtfully between her clean, bony fingers.

'Let me see . . .' she said slowly. Then suddenly she looked up, as if surprised. 'Paul, I believe this is the best thing you could have given me.' Paul squirmed, pleased but bashful. 'Now, I could do a wonderful spell with this – but I must think it out very carefully. Now, be quiet, children, and let me think – so that I can get this right.' Her fingers closed gently round the shining brass. 'This should be very good indeed. Now, quiet, please!'

The children sat like statues. Even Paul forgot to fidget. A bumble-bee came in through the window and buzzed heavily about the room. Except for this, the silence was complete.

After what seemed a long while, Miss Price opened her eyes. And then she sat up, blinking and smiling. 'There you are Paul,' she said brightly, and handed him back the bed-knob.

He took it reverently. 'Is it done?' he asked in an awestricken voice. It looked just the same to him.

'Yes, it's quite done,' Miss Price told him. 'And it's a very good spell indeed. This is something you'll enjoy. Only don't get yourselves into trouble.'

Carey and Charles were looking enviously at Paul.

'What must we do with it?' asked Charles.

'Just take it home and screw it back on the bed. But don't screw it right up. Screw it about half-way.'

'And then?'

'And then?' Miss Price smiled. 'Twist it a little and wish – and the bed will take you to wherever you want to go!'

The children gazed unbelievingly at the gleaming ball in Paul's rather grubby fingers.

'Really?' asked Carey, with a little gasp.

Miss Price was still smiling. She seemed very pleased with herself.

'Well, try it.'

'Oh, Miss Price!' breathed Carey, still gazing at the knob. 'THANK you.'

'Don't thank me,' said Miss Price, taking up her knitting again. 'Remember the conditions. One word about me and the spell is broken.'

'Oh, Miss Price!' said Carey again. She was quite overcome.

'Well, now off you go. It's getting late. As I say, don't get yourselves into trouble and don't go gallivanting around all night. There should be moderation in all things – even in magic.'

A t about ten o'clock next morning, the children were back again. Their faces were serious and their manner uncertain.

'Could I –' said Carey to the cheerful Agnes, 'could we see Miss Price?' She gave a little swallow, as if she felt nervous.

'Miss Price is engaged at the moment,' replied Agnes. 'Is there a message?'

'Well –' Carey hesitated. How much did Agnes know? She looked around at the others. Charles stepped forward.

'Could you just tell her,' he said, 'that it didn't work?'

'It didn't work?' repeated Agnes.

'Yes. Just say "It didn't work." '

'It didn't work,' repeated Agnes to herself, as if memorizing the message. She disappeared down the passage, leaving the front door open. They heard her knock. Then, after a minute, Agnes returned.

'Miss Price says will you step in.'

They were shown once more into the sitting-room. Each

chose a chair and sat on the edge of it.

'I bet she'll be angry,' whispered Paul, breaking the silence.

'Shush,' said Carey. She looked a little pale.

Suddenly the door opened and Miss Price limped in. Her foot was bandaged and she wore a carpet slipper, but she was able to walk without a stick. She looked round from face to face. 'It didn't work?' she said slowly.

'No,' replied Carey, clasping her hands together in her lap.

Miss Price sat down in the centre of the sofa. They all stared at each other in silence.

'Are you sure you did it right?'

'Yes, just what you said. We half screwed it on. Then turned it a little and wished.'

'And what happened?'

'Nothing,' said Carey. Paul's eyes, round with accusation, were fixed on Miss Price's face.

'I can't understand it,' said Miss Price, after a moment. She thought awhile. 'Have you got it with you?' she asked.

Yes, Carey had it, in a checked sponge-bag. Miss Price drew out the golden ball and gazed at it nonplussed.

'Didn't the bed move at *all*?'

'Only by Paul bouncing on it.'

'It's rusty here at the bottom,' said Miss Price.

'It was always like that,' Carey told her.

'Well, I don't know.' Miss Price stood up, gingerly putting her strained foot to the floor. 'I'll take it along and test it.'

She made a move towards the door.

'Could we watch you?'

Miss Price turned back slowly. The circle of eager eyes

seemed to hold her. They saw her hesitate. 'Please, Miss Price!' urged Carey.

'No one has seen my work-room,' said Miss Price. 'Not even Agnes.'

Carey was going to say, 'But we're in on the secret,' but she thought better of it and kept quite quiet. Their longing eyes spoke for all of them.

'Well, I'll just send Agnes off for the groceries and then I'll see.'

She went out. And it seemed an eternity before she called them. Eagerly they ran out into the passage. Miss Price was putting on a white boiler-suit. In her hand was a key. They followed her down two or three steps into a short dark passage. They heard the key turn in a well-oiled lock. Miss Price went in first, then stood aside.

'Quietly,' she said, beckoning them in. 'And careful what you touch.'

The room must at one time have been a larder. There were marble slabs and wooden shelves above the slabs. The first thing Carey noticed were the glass jars, each with its typewritten label. Miss Price, a spot of proud pink in each cheek, ran a hand along the rows.

'Toads, hares' feet, bats' wings – oh, dear!' She picked up an empty jar to which a few damp balls still clung. 'I'm out of newts' eyes!' She peered into the jar before she stood it back upon the shelf, then, taking up a pencil, she made a note on a memopad which hung upon the wall. 'They're almost impossible to get nowadays,' she said with a sigh. 'But we mustn't grumble. This is my little filing cabinet where I record results, successful – and unsuccessful, too, I'm afraid. My note-books . . .'

Carey, leaning forward, saw these were stout exercise

books, neatly labelled.

'Spells . . . Charms . . . Incantations,' she read aloud.

'And I don't suppose any of you know,' said Miss Price brightly, 'the difference between a spell and a charm.'

'I thought they were the same thing,' said Charles.

'A-ha,' replied Miss Price darkly, but her face was alight with hidden knowledge. 'I only wish a spell *were* as easy as a charm.'

She lifted a spotless piece of butter muslin, and the children peered, not without a shudder, at what appeared to be a greenish slab of meat. It lay symmetrically in a gleaming, porcelain dish and smelt faintly of chemicals.

'What is it?' asked Carey.

Miss Price eyed the dish dubiously. 'It's poisoned dragon's liver,' she said uncertainly.

'Oh,' said Carey politely.

Paul pushed up close. 'Did you poison the dragon, Miss Price? Or just the liver?' he added.

'Well,' admitted the truthful Miss Price, 'as a matter of fact, it came ready prepared. It's part of the equipment.'

'It all looks very hygienic,' ventured Carey timidly.

'My dear Carey,' said Miss Price reprovingly, 'we have progressed a *little* since the Middle Ages. Method and prophylactics have revolutionized modern witchcraft.'

Carey felt Miss Price was quoting from a book, and she longed to know a little more. 'Could I just see Lesson I?' she asked.

Miss Price glanced quickly at a pile of folders on an upper shelf and then she shook her head. 'I'm sorry, Carey. This course is absolutely confidential. "Any infringement of this regulation," ' she quoted, ' "entails a fine of not less than two hundred pounds and condemns the offender to chronic, progressively recurring, attacks of Cosmic Creepus." '

Paul looked pensive. 'It's cheaper to spit in a bus,' he announced, after some seconds of silent thought.

Gradually, the children discovered other treasures: a chart on which the signs of the zodiac were nicely touched up by Miss Price in water-colour; a sheep's skull; a chocolate box full of dried mice; herbs in bunches; a pot of growing hemlock and one of witch's bane; a small stuffed alligator which hung by two wires from the ceiling.

'What are alligators used for, Miss Price?' asked Paul.

Again Miss Price's long training in truthfulness overcame her longing to impress. 'Nothing much,' she said. 'They're out of date now. I like to have it there for the look of it.'

'It does look nice,' Paul agreed, rather enviously. He stuck his hands in his pockets. 'I had a dead hen once,' he added carelessly.

But Miss Price did not hear him. She was arranging three hazel twigs on a shelf in the form of a triangle. In the centre of this, she set the bed-knob.

'Now pass me that red notebook, just by your hand, Carey.'

'The one marked *Spells, Elementary*?'

'No, dear. The one marked *Spells, Advanced, Various*. Really, Carey,' Miss Price exclaimed, as Carey passed her a book, 'can't you read? This is *Six Easy Curses for Beginners . . .*'

'Oh, I'm sorry,' cried Carey quickly and looked again; 'this is it, I think.'

Miss Price took the book. She put on her spectacles and spent some time gazing at the open page. Picking up a pencil, she scribbled a few figures on a piece of shelf paper.

She stared at these and then she rubbed them out with the other end of the pencil.

'Miss Price –' began Paul.

'Don't interrupt me,' murmured Miss Price. 'Hellebore, henbane, aconite . . . glow-worm fire and firefly light . . . Better pull down the blinds, Carey.'

'The blinds, Miss Price?'

'Yes, over the window. Or we shan't be able to see this experiment.'

Carey pulled down the blinds and adjusted them. As the room became dark, Miss Price exclaimed: 'Now, isn't that pretty!' She sounded surprised and delighted. The children crowded round her and saw that the bed-knob glowed with a gentle light – pale as early dawn. As they watched, Miss Price twisted the knob a little and the pale light turned to rose.

'There, you see!' Miss Price said triumphantly. 'What's wrong with that, I'd like to know? Pull up the blinds again, Carey.'

Carey rolled up the blinds and Miss Price slipped an elastic band round the three hazel twigs and tidied up the notebooks.

'Come along,' she said cheerfully, opening the door. 'The spell works perfectly. Better than I hoped. I can't imagine where you went wrong.'

They followed Miss Price up the stairs, down the passage, and out through the open door into the garden, where the air was sweet with the smell of sun-warmed earth. Butterflies balanced precariously on the spears of lavender and bumble-bees hung in the foxglove bells. A milkman's cart stopped at the gate. There was a clang of bottles.

'Thank you ever so much,' said Carey. 'We'll try it again this evening. I did just what you said. I didn't screw it tight at all. I –'

'You?' said Miss Price. 'You did it, Carey?'

'Yes. I did it myself. I was very careful. I –'

'But, Carey,' said Miss Price, 'I gave the spell to Paul.'

'You mean Paul should've –?'

'Of course. Paul should have done it. No wonder it didn't work.'

Slowly, wonderingly, a grin of ecstasy began to stretch itself across Paul's face. His eyes gleamed moistly with an almost holy joy.

Carey and Charles looked at him as though they had never seen him before.

'Well?' said Miss Price, rather sharply.

Charles found his voice. 'He's sort of young,' he pointed out, 'for so much responsibility.'

But Miss Price was firm. 'The younger the better, as I know to my cost. Now run along, children.' She turned away, but almost immediately she turned back again, lowering her voice: 'Oh, by the way, I meant to tell you something else. You know I said the spell was better than I hoped. Well, if you twist it one way the bed will take you where you want, in the present. Twist it the other way and the bed will take you back into the past.'

'Oh, Miss Price!' exclaimed Carey.

'What about the future?' asked Charles.

Miss Price looked at him as the bus conductor looks when you ask for a ticket to a place off the bus route. Charles blushed, and churned up the gravel path with the toe of his shoe.

'Now, remember what I said,' went on Miss Price. 'Have a good time, keep to the rules, and *allow for the bed*.'

She turned to the milkman, who had been waiting patiently by the step. 'Half a pint, please, Mr Bisselthwaite, and my butter.'

*I*t was hard to get through the rest of the day, but evening came at last; by the time it was Paul's bedtime, anticipation had made them tired and excitement had grown stale.

'Look here, Paul,' said Carey suddenly, as Paul was brushing his teeth. 'You wouldn't go and do it by yourself. You'll lie still till Charles and I come to bed, won't you?'

Paul looked at her over the slowly revolving brush.

'If you went off on that bed by yourself,' continued Carey, 'and it went wrong, no one could save you. You might get stuck in the past or anything.'

Paul spat into the hole in the basin. He watched the hole, and then, carefully, he spat again. He felt aggrieved: from the moment he had screwed on the bed-knob, after getting back from Miss Price's, Carey and Charles had not let him out of their sight for an instant. It was his bed after all, and, what was more, his bed-knob. They might have let him have a trial run, just to the bottom of the garden, say, and back.

He hadn't wanted to go far, but he had wanted to know if it really worked.

'You see, Paul,' went on Carey, 'suppose Elizabeth came upstairs with your supper, and the bed was gone. What then? We've got to be very careful. It may seem deceitful but we *did* promise Miss Price. You can't go tearing about on the bed in broad daylight, and things like that.'

Paul rinsed his mouth and swallowed the water, as was his custom.

'Do you see, Paul? We've got to wait until they're all in bed. Come here, and I'll comb your hair while it's wet.'

They followed him into his bedroom. They sat on the bed. They all looked at the bed-knob, just above Paul's right ear; it looked just like the other three.

'I bet it doesn't work,' said Charles. 'I bet you anything.'

'Shush,' said Carey, as Elizabeth came in with their supper on a tray.

'Don't spill it on the sheet, now,' she said, panting. 'And bring the tray down, Miss Carey, please, it's my evening out.'

'Your evening out?' repeated Carey. She began to smile.

'Nothing funny in that, I hope,' said Elizabeth tartly. 'I've earned it. And no tricks, now, your aunt's not herself. She's gone to bed.'

'Gone to bed?' echoed Carey again. She caught back the rest of her smile just in time. Elizabeth looked at her curiously.

'No tricks, now,' she repeated. 'There's something funny about you children. Butter wouldn't melt in your mouths, but I'm not so sure.'

They heard her sigh on the landing. They heard her turn the corner. Then they kicked off their slippers and danced.

Noiselessly, tensely, breathlessly, they gyrated and whirled and leapt, then, panting, they fell on to Paul's bed.

'Where shall we go?' whispered Carey, her eyes shining.

'Let's try a South Sea island,' said Charles.

Paul bit deeply into his bread. His cheeks bulged and his jaws moved slowly. He was the calmest of the three.

'The Rocky Mountains,' suggested Carey.

'The South Pole,' said Charles.

'The Pyramids.'

'Tibet.'

'The moon.'

'Where would you like to go, Paul?' asked Carey suddenly. Happiness had made her unselfish.

Paul swallowed his mouthful of bread and butter. 'I'd like to go to the Natural History Museum.'

'Oh, Paul,' said Carey.

'Not that kind of place. You can go there any time.'

'I'd like to see the Big Flea in the Natural History Museum,' said Paul. He remembered how Carey and Charles had gone with an uncle, without him, when he, Paul, had been in bed with a cold.

'It was only a model. Think of another place, Paul. You can have first turn, as it's your bed. But somewhere nice.'

'I'd like to go to London,' said Paul.

'But you can go to London almost any time,' Charles reminded him.

'I'd like to go to London to see my mother.'

'Don't say "my mother." She's our mother, too.'

'I'd like to see her,' repeated Paul simply.

'Well, we'd like to see her,' admitted Carey. 'But she'd be kind of surprised.'

'I'd like to see my mother.' Paul's lips began to tremble

and his eyes filled with tears. Carey looked worried.

'Paul,' she tried to explain, 'when you get a thing as magic as this, you don't make that kind of wish, like seeing your mother and going to museums and things, you wish for something absolutely extraordinary. Don't you see, Paul? Try again.'

Paul's face turned crimson and the tears rolled out of his eyes and down his cheeks.

'I'd like to see my mother, or the Big Flea.' He was trying not to sob aloud. He closed his lips and his chest heaved up and down.

'Oh, dear,' said Carey desperately. She stared down at her shoes.

'Let him have his turn,' Charles suggested in a patient voice. 'We can go somewhere else afterwards.'

'But don't you see –' began Carey. 'Oh, all right,' she added. 'Come on. Get on the bed, Charles.' She began to feel excited again.

'Let's all hold on to the rails. Better tuck in that bit of blanket. Now, Paul, take hold of the knob – gently. Here, I'll blow your nose. Now, are you ready?'

Paul knelt up, facing the head of the bed and the wall. He had his hand on the knob. 'What shall I say?'

'Say mother's address. Say "I wish to be at No 38 Markham Square" and twist.'

'I wish to be –' Paul's voice sounded thick. He cleared his throat.

'At No 38,' prompted Carey.

'At No 38.'

'Markham Square.'

'Markham Square.'

Nothing happened. There was an awful moment of

suspense, then Carey added quickly, 'SW3.'

'SW3,' repeated Paul.

It was horrible. It was a swooshing rush, as if the world had changed into a cinema film run too quickly. A jumble that was almost fields, almost trees, almost streets, almost houses, but nothing long enough. The bed rocked. They clung to the railings. The bed-clothes whipped round Carey and Charles who clung to the foot, blinding them, choking them. A great seasick lurch. Then Bang . . . Bump . . . Clang . . . and a sliding scrape.

They had arrived.

They felt shaken and breathless. Slowly Carey unwound

a blanket from her neck and head. Her mouth was full of fluff. The eiderdown was blown tight round Charles and hung through the brass rails of the bed. Paul was still kneeling on the pillow. His face was scarlet and his hair was blown upright.

'Gosh,' said Charles, after a moment. He looked about him. They were indeed in Markham Square. The bed had come to rest neatly along the pavement, overlapping the kerb. There was No 38 with its black front door, its chequered steps, and the area railing. Charles felt extraordinarily conspicuous. The bed was so very much a bed and the street so very much a street, and there was Paul crossing the pavement in his bare feet to ring the front door bell. Paul, in his pyjamas and with such untidy hair, standing on mother's front steps in broad daylight – a warm, rich evening light, but none the less broad daylight.

Charles prayed for the door to open quickly. He was by nature extremely retiring.

A red bus rolled by at the end of the square. For the moment, the pavement was empty.

'Ring again,' he cried fervently. Paul rang again.

They heard the echo of the bell in the basement, a polite, regretful, empty sound. The dark windows stared blankly.

'There's no one at home,' said Carey when they had waited a minute or two longer. She uncurled her legs. 'Mother must have gone out to dinner,' she announced, standing up. 'Well, we'll have to wait. Let's tidy the bed.'

As they made the bed, drawing up the blankets, turning back the sheets, plumping up the pillows, Charles marvelled at Carey's and Paul's lack of concern. Didn't they think it odd, he wondered, to be making a bed there in a London street? He glanced longingly towards the area steps. 'Shall we try the back door?' he suggested: anything to be away from the bed, and down below the level of the pavement. He couldn't go far because he hadn't any shoes on.

They crept down the area steps. They rattled and pulled at the tradesmen's door. It was locked. They peered in at the kitchen window. A cup and saucer lay on the drying-board; the rest of the kitchen was curiously tidy and deathly still. The window was fastened. Even breaking it would have done no good. It was barred against burglars.

'We must just sit on the bed and wait,' sighed Carey.

'Not on the bed,' said Charles hastily. 'Let's stay down here, where no one can see us,' he added.

They all squeezed together on the bottom step, facing the dustbin. The area smelt of wet tea leaves and the step was cold.

'I don't call this much of an adventure,' said Charles.

'Nor do I,' agreed Carey. 'It was Paul's idea.'

It grew darker. Looking upwards, they saw that the light was draining quickly from the street above. There was mist in the air.

They began to hear passers-by. The footsteps always paused at No 38, and the children, listening, realized how much grown-ups think alike. They nearly all said, with deep surprise, 'How funny! A bed!' or 'A bed! How funny!' Always they heard the word 'Bed. Bed, bed, bed,' and footsteps. Once Charles spoke for them. As he heard the footsteps pause, he said aloud. 'How funny, a bed!' It was almost dark then, and a form peered down at them over the area railings. 'Some children,' muttered a voice, as if explaining to a second person. As the footsteps died away, Charles called after them, 'And a bed.'

'Don't Charles, it's rude. You'll get us into trouble.'

It became quite dark, a darkness laced with mist.

'River fog,' said Charles, 'and if you ask me, I think mother's gone away for the week-end.'

Paul was already asleep against Carey's shoulder. Carey had a sudden brain-wave.

'I know!' she exclaimed. 'Let's get into the bed! It's quite dark now. If it's foggy enough, no one will see us.'

They went up the steps again and crossed the pavement. Ah! It was good to crawl under the blankets and to pull up the eiderdown. Above them the sky looked greyish between the steep black roofs. The stars had disappeared.

'I honestly don't call this much of an adventure,' whispered Charles.

'I know,' Carey replied. 'But it's the first time. We'll get better at it.'

Between them, Paul breathed deeply, exuding a pleasant warmth.

Carey must have been asleep for some time when the shock came. At first, shaken out of a dream, she lay quite still. Damp darkness . . . her legs felt pinioned. Where was she? Then she remembered.

'Please!' she cried, with an agonized squeak. The fog had deepened. She could see nothing.

There was a hoarse gasp. 'Well, I'll be –'

'Please,' cried Carey again, interrupting. '*Please* get off my foot.'

A light flashed on, a terrifying dazzling circle; shining straight in their eyes as it did, it felt like a searchlight.

The gruff voice said again, 'Well, I'll be blowed – kids!'

The weight lifted itself and thankfully Carey curled back her legs, blinking at the glare. She knew suddenly, without being able to see a thing, that behind that light was a policeman. She felt a policeman, large and tall and fat and creaking.

He switched off his torch. 'Kids!' he said again in a surprised voice. Then he became stern. 'Can't 'ave this, you know,' he breathed heavily, 'can't 'ave beds, like this, in the street. Danger to the public. Caught me on the shin, this bed did. A street's no place for beds. Where's your mother?'

'I don't know,' said Carey in a low voice.

'Speak up,' said the policeman. 'What's your name?'

'Carey Wilson.'

On went the light again and out came a notebook. Again the policeman sat down. The bed creaked, but Carey's toes were out of reach.

'Address?'

Charles sat up sleepily. 'What?' he said.

Carey had a sudden vision of Aunt Beatrice's face, the tight lips, the pink-rimmed eyes. She thought of her mother, worried, upset. Letters, policemen, complaints, fines, prison.

'Look,' said Carey, 'I'm terribly sorry we hurt your shin. If you'd just move, we'll take the bed away and then you won't be troubled any more. We'll take it right away. Really.'

'This 'ere's an iron bed,' said the policeman. 'This 'ere bed's good and heavy.'

'We can take it,' urged Carey. 'We brought it here. We have a way of taking it.'

'I don't see no way of taking this bed anywhere – not in this fog.'

'If you'd just move a moment,' said Carey, 'we'll show you.'

'Not so fast, miss.' The policeman was getting into his

stride. 'I'm not moving anywhere, just at present. Where did you bring this 'ere bed FROM?'

Carey hesitated. Trouble – that was what they were heading for. She thought again of Aunt Beatrice. And of Miss Price – oh, Miss Price, that was almost the worst of all; to tell about Miss Price would be the end of everything – yet no good ever came of lying.

'Well,' said Carey, trying to think quickly.

'We brought it from my room,' put in Paul suddenly.

'Oh,' said the policeman heavily. He had adopted a slightly sarcastic tone to hide his bewilderment. 'And where might your room be?'

'Next to Carey's,' said Paul. 'At the end of the passage.'

The policeman, who had switched off his torch, switched it on again into Paul's eyes. Carey and Charles, who up to that moment had thought little or nothing of Paul's looks, suddenly realized that he had a face like an angel. Two little wings could have been tied to his back and they would not have looked out of place. Even a halo would have suited Paul.

The policeman switched out his light. 'Poor little shaver,' he muttered, 'dragging 'im round London at this time o' night.'

This was more than Carey could stand. 'Why,' she cried indignantly, 'it's all his fault. It was all his idea –'

'Now, now,' said the policeman. 'That's enough. What I want to know is, where did you get this 'ere bed? What part o' London, to be exact?'

'It didn't come from London at all,' said Charles.

'Then WHERE did it come from?' thundered the policeman.

'From Bedfordshire,' said Carey.

The policeman stood up. Carey heard him catch his breath angrily.

'Joke, eh?'

'Not at all,' said Carey.

'You mean to tell me you brought this 'ere bed all the way up from Bedfordshire?'

'Yes,' said Carey.

The policeman sighed. Carey felt him trying to be patient. 'By train?'

'No,' said Carey.

'Then how, may I ask?'

'Well –' said Carey. She thought again of Miss Price. 'Well, we can't really tell you.'

'You tell me how you brought this bed up from Bedfordshire, or you come along with me to the police station – where you're coming anyway,' he added.

'All right,' said Carey, feeling the tears sting into her eyes. 'I'll tell you. If you want to know, we brought it up by magic.'

There was a silence. A terrific silence. Carey wondered if the policeman was going to hit her with his truncheon, but when at last he spoke, he spoke very quietly. 'Oh, you did, did you? By magic. Now I'll tell you something. You've 'eard of the law, 'aven't you? Well, the law is just and, in a manner of speaking, the law is kind, but there's one thing the law can't be –' He took a deep breath. 'The law can't be made fun of. Now, all three of you, get out of that there bed and come along with me to the station!'

With a sinking heart Carey drew her legs from under the blankets.

'I haven't any shoes on,' said Charles.

There was no reply. The policeman seemed drawn away

from them in spirit, wrapped in lofty silence.

'Nor has Paul,' pointed out Carey. 'You'll have to carry him,' she added.

THE POLICE STATION

I t was not a long walk, but it was a trying one for
Charles in his stockinged feet. Never before had he
realized quite how many different kinds of surface go
to make a London street. Paul rode majestically in the
policeman's arms, sharing the policeman's vast aloofness.
Carey walked in dark depression. Every step they took away
from the bed decreased their chances of escape. Prison!
'Oh,' she thought in desperation, 'why didn't I tell Paul to
wish the bed away with us, policeman and all?' But that
might have been even more complicated; arriving back at
Aunt Beatrice's with a policeman; trying to smuggle a
policeman out of Paul's bedroom, to smuggle a policeman
out of the house . . . and he wasn't at all the kind of
policeman who would lend himself to being smuggled
anywhere. There was, Carey realized unhappily, practically
no reliable method of getting rid of unwanted policemen.
No, bad as it was, this possibly was the lesser of the two evils.

They were in the police station almost before they knew it.

There was a long counter, a green-shaded light, and a grey-haired policeman without a hat. He had a tired, thin face, a soldier's face. Carey felt herself trembling.

'Well, Sergeant?' said the grey-haired officer wearily. 'I thought we were through for tonight.'

'Well, sir, these 'ere children, sir. Thought I'd better bring 'em along. Out in the street, with a bed, sir. Obstructing traffic – public nuisance as it were.'

The inspector was reaching for his cap which hung on a peg.

'Well, take their names and addresses and get hold of the parents.' He paused and turned slowly. 'Out in the street with a what?'

'With a bed, sir.'

'A BED!'

'Yes, sir, an iron bed like, with knobs on.'

The inspector looked wonderingly at Carey. Suddenly Carey knew she liked his face. She liked the screwed-up look of his eyes and the tired lines of his mouth. She wished terribly that she had not been brought before him as a criminal. He looked at all three of them for a moment longer, then he addressed the sergeant.

'Where is the bed now?'

'There in the street, sir. Markham Square.'

'Better send the van to collect the bed.' He sighed. 'And hand these children over to Mrs Watkins till you get hold of the parents. I'm dead beat, sergeant. Court at 9.30, don't forget. I'll need you and Sergeant Coles.'

'Yes, sir. Good night, sir.'

As the inspector passed, on his way to the door, he glanced again at the children. 'He would have talked to us,' Carey thought, 'if he hadn't been so tired.' She felt very frightened. If only someone had scolded them she would have felt less frightened. She felt as if something bigger than a person had got hold of them, something enormous, something of which the policemen themselves stood in awe. She guessed it was the 'law' – the law that 'could not be made fun of.'

The sergeant was speaking into a telephone which hung from a bracket on the wall.

'Yes, three of 'em . . . No – just overnight . . . No, 'e's gone off. Dead beat, 'e was . . . Cup o' tea? Not if you got it made, I wouldn't . . . Righty oh.'

He brought out his notebook and wrote down their mother's address. 'Why,' he said, after some minutes of silent and ponderous calculation. 'You was right by your own house.'

'Mother's away,' said Carey quickly, hoping to stop him ringing up.

'Did you say you brought the bed up from Bedfordshire?'

'We did,' said Carey. 'The house is locked up.'

The policeman was busy writing. 'Right by your own house,' he murmured. 'That's different.'

'Well,' he said, closing his notebook. 'Come along with me for the time being.'

He took the children down a passage, out of a back door into a pitch-dark courtyard. 'Mind where you tread,' he told them.

Paul took Carey's hand. 'Are we going to prison?' he whispered.

'I don't know,' Carey whispered back. 'I think so.'

'How many years,' asked Paul, 'will they keep us in prison?'

'I don't know,' said Carey, 'not many.'

'Come on,' said the sergeant. They felt he was holding a door open. They squeezed past his stomach into another passage. They were indoors again. The sergeant switched on a light. 'Mrs Watkins,' he called.

Mrs Watkins was a bustling kind of woman, a cross – Carey thought – between a cloak-room attendant and a nurse. She wore a white apron and a red woollen cardigan over it. She took them into a room in which there was a bed – like a hospital bed, thought Carey – two imitation leather armchairs, a table, and an aspidistra in a pot. She bustled Paul on to the bed and covered him with a blanket. Then she turned to Charles and Carey. 'Cocoa or tea?' she asked them.

Carey hesitated. 'Whichever's easiest for you,' she said politely.

'The sergeant's having tea.'

'Well, tea if you've got it made,' said Carey timidly. 'Thank you very much,' she added.

Mrs Watkins stared at Carey for a minute. 'Lost, are you?' she asked curiously.

Carey, sitting on the edge of the imitation leather armchair, smiled uneasily. 'Not exactly.'

'Up to mischief?' asked Mrs Watkins.

Carey blushed and tears came into her eyes. 'Not exactly,' she stammered.

'Well,' said Mrs Watkins kindly, 'you sit there quiet and be good children and you'll have a nice cup o' tea.'

'Thank you,' murmured Carey indistinctly.

As the door closed behind Mrs Watkins and the key turned in the lock, Carey burst into tears. Charles stared at her miserably, and Paul, sitting up in bed with interest, asked, 'What are you crying for, Carey?'

'This is all so awful,' wept Carey, trying at the same time to staunch her tears with her handkerchief.

'I don't think it's so awful,' said Paul. 'I like this prison.'

Charles glared at him. 'Only because you're going to have a cup of tea, and you know you're not allowed tea at home.'

'No,' said Paul rather vaguely, 'I like prisons like this.'

'Well, it isn't even a prison. It's a police station.'

'Oh,' said Paul. He gazed about the room, but a little less happily.

'Paul,' said Carey, some time later, when they had drunk their tea and Mrs Watkins had left them alone again, 'I told you this was a stupid kind of wish. I tried to warn you. It would have been better to go back into the Middle Ages or anything than this. This is worse than anything that has ever happened to us. We've lost the bed. The policeman will ring up mother. Mother will be terribly worried. The law may get her too. Aunt Beatrice will know. They'll make us explain everything. Miss Price will get into trouble. We shall have broken our promise. It will be the end of magic. And nobody will ever trust us again . . .'

Paul looked grave.

'Do you see, Paul?' Carey's voice sounded as if she were going to cry again. 'And it's Charles and me who'll get the blame. They'll say we led you into it. That we're old enough to know better. Do you understand?'

Paul brightened perceptibly. 'Yes,' he said.

'We're locked in here. And there isn't anything we can do.'

She broke off. Suddenly outside in the courtyard there was a screech of brakes. They heard the running engine of a car, and voices shouting.

'They're bringing someone else in!' exclaimed Paul excitedly.

Charles went up to the window but he dared not disturb the blind. 'They'll see us,' he said.

'I know what,' cried Carey. 'Switch out this light.'

Charles switched off the light by the door. Then, in the darkness, he tugged a corner of the blind. It flew up with a rattle. A pinkish light, faint but clear, shone inwards on the room.

'It's dawn,' said Charles wonderingly. 'Morning. The fog's gone. We've been away all night.' He stared down into the courtyard.

'I say, Carey –'

'What?'

'They're not bringing anyone in. It's –' He paused excitedly. 'Carey, it's the bed!'

Carey leapt out of her chair and Paul threw off the blanket. They raced to the window. They watched, in that dim early light, two policemen lift the bed from the van. They heard the legs scrape as it was dragged across the cobble-stones. They saw the policemen push it up against the wall. Then both men stood, rubbing the strain out of their hands, and staring at the bed. They laughed. 'I could do with a nap meself,' said one as they walked away indoors. Then the courtyard became silent.

'If we could get to it –' breathed Charles.

'If –' said Carey.

The pale light shone softly on their faces as, longingly, they stared out through the bars.

At about nine o'clock next morning, the sergeant and the inspector faced each other across the inspector's desk. The sergeant was standing. His hat was in his hand and his face was very red.

'. . . and that's all I know, sir,' the sergeant was saying.

'But how did they get away?' asked the inspector. 'I'm afraid I don't follow you, sergeant. How did they get into the yard, to start with?'

'Well, Mrs Watkins took 'em down, sir, to see my garden.'

'To see your garden?' repeated the inspector in a surprised voice.

'Them dahlias, sir, in pots, at the end of the yard, sir. Mrs Watkins calls 'em my garden. I got some sweet peas, sir, too – coming up nicely, the sweet peas are.'

'I didn't know you were a horticulturist, sergeant.' The inspector spoke rather coldly. 'And then?'

'Mrs Watkins, she quite took to those kids, sir. She thought they'd like to see the bird, sir, too.'

'The bird?'

'I got a canary down there, sir. I was putting it out, like, in the sun, early this morning.'

'Have you got anything else down there in the yard?'

The sergeant shuffled his feet.

'Well, sir, only the silkworms.'

The inspector glanced out of the window, pursing up his mouth in a rather peculiar way as if he were trying to keep it still.

'And you left the children alone in the yard?' he asked sternly.

'Well, sir, the gate was locked, sir. Roberts was on duty outside. I'd just slipped in the passage to sip a cup o' tea Mrs Watkins 'ad there waiting –'

'Well, go on. How long were you sipping this tea?'

'No time at all, sir. I just took the cup like from Mrs Watkins, put in a bit of sugar, stirred it, and came right out to the door –'

'And then –?'

'Well, I couldn't see the children. I thought at first they was round be'ind the pillars.' The sergeant wiped his face with his handkerchief. 'But no,' he added.

'They'd gone?'

'Yes, sir, they'd gone.'

'And the bed, too.'

'Yes, sir, and the bed too. We searched the premises. The yard gate was still padlocked. Roberts said he 'adn't seen nothing.'

The inspector stared at his finger-nails. 'Very peculiar. Mrs Watkins bears out your story?'

'Yes, sir.'

'Mrs Watkins took to them, you say?'

'Yes, sir. They were nice kids, sir, well brought up. I got sort of sore with 'em last night. 'Urt my leg on that there bed of theirs. But they weren't bad, not at 'eart they weren't.'

The inspector leaned back in his chair. 'You took to them yourself, in fact?'

'Not last night I didn't. But this morning – well, sir, they were so pleased like to see my little bird.'

'You regretted, perhaps,' said the inspector slowly, fixing the sergeant with his eye, 'having brought them in at all.'

The sergeant stared back at the inspector. His eyes became very round and blue in his red face. He opened his mouth with a gasp. 'You think I went and let them out, sir?' Then his fat face became stern and dignified. He swallowed. 'I wouldn't do a thing like that. I know my duty, sir.' He looked hurt and stared at a spot on the wall above the inspector's head.

The inspector smiled. 'I'm sorry, sergeant, if I've mis-judged you. But you've told me a very tall story, you know. If the front gate is locked, there's absolutely no way out of the yard.'

'I know, sir.'

'And there's the business of the bed . . .'

'Yes, sir,' said the sergeant.

'These children couldn't be considered in any way as delinquents. They were just having some prank, isn't that so?'

'Yes, sir.' Suddenly a curious half-shy look came into the sergeant's eyes. He twisted his hat round in his hands. He looked at the inspector as if he hardly dared put his thought into words.

'Something just occurred to me, sir.' The sergeant was blushing.

'Well?'

'The little girl, when I asked 'er 'ow she brought the bed up from Bedfordshire . . .'

'Yes?'

The sergeant dropped his voice. 'She said she brought it up by magic.'

For a moment the inspector did not speak, then, 'Really, sergeant –' he said weakly.

The sergeant's blush became deeper. 'I know, sir,' he said humbly.

'Really, sergeant,' went on the inspector, standing up and beginning to gather together the papers he would need in court. 'You're a grown man, now. You must curb these fancies.'

CAREY HAS AN IDEA

I t was with a feeling of great relief that the children found themselves back again in Paul's bedroom. Carey and Charles barely had time to wash themselves and to dress Paul before Elizabeth sounded the gong for breakfast. Paul nearly fell asleep over his porridge, and Carey and Charles felt guilty when, later on, Elizabeth thanked them for having made the beds they hadn't slept in. Their adventure did not seem like a dream, but it seemed as if they had been away for much longer than one night, and all of them felt very sleepy.

'Let's go down and see Miss Price this morning,' suggested Carey, 'and this afternoon let's go up to the hayloft and sleep till tea-time.'

They found Miss Price kneeling at her flower border, planting. She wore a large straw hat and a canvas apron with pockets. It was a lovely day and the scented garden lay a-dream in the blazing warmth of the sun.

'Well,' said Miss Price, sitting back and staring anxiously

at their flushed, perspiring faces, 'did it work?'

'Yes,' said Carey. 'It worked like magic – I mean, like a charm – I mean . . . Oh, Miss Price, it *did* work.' She flung herself down on the grass beside Miss Price.

'Did you enjoy yourselves?' asked Miss Price, rather anxiously. 'Paul looks as though he can hardly keep his eyes open.'

Carey pulled up a little tuft of the sweet-smelling lawn.

'Well, we didn't exactly *enjoy* ourselves,' she admitted, and tried to push the tuft back again.

'You didn't!' exclaimed Miss Price. She looked worried.

Then out came the whole story. The children often interrupted each other and sometimes they spoke in chorus, but gradually Miss Price pieced the pattern together. She became graver and graver as they described their adventures with the law, and looked aghast when she heard they had actually been taken to the police station. She looked sad when Charles told her how the prison van had brought the bed into the yard and how they had stared at it through the barred window, but she brightened considerably when they got to the bit about the sergeant's garden. Carey copied Mrs Watkins's voice saying, 'Well, pop down and look at the bird then, but don't you touch them dahlias.' They didn't have to describe the rest. Miss Price knew too well what would happen once they were in reach of the bed. 'Did anyone see you go?' she asked.

'No,' said Carey, 'that's when the sergeant went inside for his cup of tea.'

'Did the bed go at once?'

'Yes, like a flash. The second that Paul wished. We'd hardly got on it.'

'Well,' said Miss Price thoughtfully, 'let's hope they *don't* ring up your mother.'

'Mother would say it couldn't have been us,' pointed out Charles. 'She'd know we couldn't have been in London.'

'That's true, Charles,' agreed Carey. 'And Aunt Beatrice would say at once that we were here. We couldn't have been in London, possibly.'

Paul looked bewildered. 'Then where were we?' he asked.

'Oh Paul!' exclaimed Carey impatiently. She turned her back on him and watched Miss Price, who had begun once more to dig holes with the trowel. 'What are you planting, Miss Price?'

'Edelweiss,' said Miss Price absently. She sighed. 'Well, all's well that ends well. You were lucky. It might have been worse, a good deal worse.'

Carey watched Miss Price insert a silvery plant in the hole, and Charles rolled over sleepily to observe an aeroplane flying across the peaceful sky.

'I thought edelweiss only grew above the snow-line,' Carey remarked wonderingly.

Miss Price became rather pink and pursed up her lips. 'It grows quite well in my garden,' she said shortly.

Carey was silent. After she had thought awhile, she said carelessly, 'Are you showing anything in the flower show, Miss Price?'

Miss Price's colour deepened. 'I might show a rose.'

'A new rose?' asked Carey interestedly.

'No, a big one,' said Miss Price.

'Can we see it?' asked Carey.

'Well, it's still in bud,' said Miss Price unwillingly.

'Could we see the bud?'

'Oh dear, Carey,' cried Miss Price, suddenly exasperated, 'I'm sure it's your lunch-time.'

'Not till one o'clock,' said Carey reassuringly. 'Miss Price.'

'Well?'

'If anyone was going in for a flower show, would it be fair for them to use magic?'

Miss Price flattened out the earth round the plant with the trowel. She banged it rather hard. 'Perfectly fair,' she said.

Carey was silent. Paul lay on his face, watching an earwig in the grass. He held one eye open with his finger. He was very sleepy. Miss Price dug another hole.

'What about the people who can't do magic?' asked Carey after a while.

'What about the people who can buy special fertilizers?' retorted Miss Price, jamming the plant in the hole upside down, and then pulling it out again. 'What about the people with hothouses?' She shook the plant savagely to get the earth off the leaves. 'What about the people who can afford expensive gardeners?' She sat back on her heels and glared at Carey. 'How am I to compete with Lady Warbuckle, for instance?'

Carey blinked her eyes. 'I only wondered,' she said timidly.

'I worked for my knowledge,' said Miss Price grimly, starting on another hole. Her face was very red.

'Miss Price,' began Carey again after a while.

'Well?'

'Why don't you make a whole lot of golden sovereigns?'

'Of golden sovereigns?'

'Yes, sacks and sacks of them. Then you could buy hothouses and fertilizers and things.'

Miss Price sighed. She pushed her hat back a little from

her forehead. 'I have tried to explain to you, Carey, how difficult witchcraft is, but you still think I just have to wave a wand for anything to happen. Have you ever heard of a rich witch?'

'No,' admitted Carey, 'I can't say I have.'

'Well, I'll tell you why. Money is the hardest thing of all to make. That's why most witches live in hovels. Not because they like it. I was fortunate enough,' she added primly, 'to have a little annuity left me by my dear mother.'

'Aren't there any spells for making money?'

'Dozens. But you can't get the ingredients. What people don't realize,' went on Miss Price, 'is that there are very few spells that can be done without paraphernalia. You must, if you understand, have something to turn into something and something to turn it *with*.'

'Yes,' said Carey, 'I see.' And it was indeed as clear as daylight to her.

'And there are very few spells I know by heart,' admitted Miss Price. 'I have to have time to look them up. And quiet. I can't be fussed.' She took up her trowel again. 'If I'm fussed, everything goes straight out of my head. Now you must wake up those boys. There's the church clock striking three quarters.'

Carey got up unwillingly. 'I wish,' she said, 'you'd come with us on the next adventure.'

'Well,' said Miss Price, 'it depends on where you go. If I came, I'd like it a good deal better arranged than last night was, for instance.'

'We'd let you choose,' offered Carey.

'Well,' said Miss Price brightly. 'We could all plan it together, couldn't we?' She seemed flustered and pleased at the same time. 'But not tonight. Beauty sleep tonight . . .'

The South Sea island idea came to Carey in the hayloft. She had awakened first and lay sleepily staring at the patch of blue sky through the open door, breathing the sweet smell of the dried apples left over from last year.

'What a pity,' she thought, as she stared at the sky, 'that we have to go everywhere at night. There are heaps of places I'd like to see, but in daylight.' Then slowly she remembered that daylight was not the same all over the world, that the earth was slowly turning, that if you could travel fast enough – in a magic bed, for instance – you might catch up with the sun. The idea gradually took shape and became such an unbearably exciting possibility that she had to wake Charles.

They discussed it at long length, all that evening between tea and bedtime, and the very next morning they tackled Miss Price. Apart from liking her, Carey thought she might perhaps feel safer if Miss Price came along too; a little extra magic couldn't come amiss and the police station episode had had its frightening moments.

Miss Price was a little alarmed at first at the distance.

'Oh, I can't go gadding about the Pacific at my age, Carey. I like what I'm used to. You'd better go by yourselves.'

'Oh, do come, Miss Price,' Carey begged her. 'You needn't gad about. You can just sit in the sun and rest your ankle. It would do you good.'

'Oh, it would be wonderful, Miss Price. Just think – bananas, bread-fruit, pineapples, mangoes! You could come on the broomstick.'

'The broomstick can only do about five miles at a stretch,' objected Miss Price, but her eyes lit up at the thought of a bread-fruit cutting in a pot.

'Then you can come with us on the bed. There's heaps of room. Do, do, Miss Price!'

Miss Price wavered. 'It would be a change,' she admitted.

'Couldn't we go tonight?'

'Tonight!' Miss Price looked startled.

'Well, why not? We slept last night.'

Miss Price succumbed. 'Well,' she said hesitatingly, 'if you slept last night . . .'

Paul was a little mystified by the South Sea island idea, but when Carey and Charles had explained to him the wonders of a coral reef, he too, became agreeable, but insisted on being allowed to take his bucket and spade.

Miss Price got out an atlas and an encyclopaedia, and they searched for islands whose dawn would correspond with sunset in England, where European night became Pacific day. They did sums and calculations on the backs of envelopes, and at last they decided on an island called Ueepe. It was not marked on the map, but it was mentioned in the encyclopaedia as an island yet to be explored. It had been sighted among others mentioned from the sailing ship *Lucia Cavorta* in 1809 and was spoken of by this name by natives on the island of Panu, 450 miles distant, and was said to be uninhabited.

'We'll have the whole place to ourselves,' exclaimed Carey delightedly. 'We could even rename it.'

As it would hardly be possible for Miss Price to sneak into Aunt Beatrice's house so late in the evening and make her way up to Paul's bedroom, it was decided that Miss Price was to come to the window on her broomstick at dusk, and that the children would let her in.

Charles mended Paul's spade for him, and they also found a butterfly net, 'which might do for shrimping or anything.'

The children undressed and had their baths just as usual. Because it was one of those nights when Elizabeth wanted to talk about her sister's little boy's operation, she followed them about from bathroom to bedroom, telling them the well-known details. They knew that later, when she served Aunt Beatrice's dinner, she would sigh and say that she was 'worn out getting those children to bed.'

But she went at last, stumping down the stairs, and Carey and Charles slipped from their room into Paul's. Paul was asleep, so they sat on his bed and talked in whispers until it began to grow dark. Then they went to the window and watched for Miss Price. Charles was the first to spy her, flying low in the shadows of the cedars. The broomstick had a slightly overloaded look and swayed against the window-sill as a dinghy bumps against a ship's side. It was difficult getting Miss Price in at the window. She was carrying a string bag, a book, and an umbrella, and she dared not let go of the broomstick until her legs were safely over the sill. She knocked her hat off on the lower part of the sash and Carey, picking it up, found that it was a sun helmet. 'My father's,' explained Miss Price, in a loud whisper, panting after her exertions, 'the one he had in Poona in '99. It has mosquito netting round the brim.'

Carey peered at it dimly in the fading light, as it swung upon her finger. It smelt strongly of naphtha. 'I don't think there are any mosquitoes in the South Seas,' she whispered back.

'Well,' replied Miss Price briskly, tying the string bag to the foot of the bed with Paul's dressing-gown cord. 'Preven-

tion is better than cure. Better slip the umbrella under the mattress, Charles. And my book, too, please.'

It was so dark now that they could hardly see each other's faces. There was no moon, and the cedar boughs were but dim shadows against a grey sky.

Carey wondered suddenly whether they ought to have dressed again. She hadn't thought of it, somehow. Now, it seemed too late. The dark room was full of bustle. Paul was waking as Charles heaved at the mattress to stow away the book and umbrella.

'What do you want?' he asked sleepily.

Carey flew to his side. 'Put your dressing-gown on,' she whispered. 'It's time to go.'

'To go where?' asked Paul, in his normal voice.

'Shush,' whispered Carey. 'To the South Sea island. The coral reef, you remember?'

'But it's so dark,' objected Paul.

'It will be daylight there.' She was putting his arms in the sleeves of his dressing-gown. 'There's a good boy,' she praised him. 'You've got to say "I wish to go to Ueepe." Here's your net and bucket and spade. I'll take them for you. Kneel up, Paul.'

Paul knelt up, facing the head of the bed. Miss Price was firmly tucking in the blankets. She laid her broomstick under the eiderdown. Then they all took their places. Miss Price sat next to Paul and Charles and Carey held on at the foot.

Paul put his hand on the knob. Then he turned round. 'It makes me feel sick, when the bed goes,' he announced.

'Oh, Paul,' whispered Carey. 'It's only a minute. You can bear it. Miss Price has a nice picnic in her bag,' she added as an inducement. 'Go on. Twist.'

Paul twisted. The bed gave a sickening lurch. The night seemed to turn blue, a blue that glittered like a flying tinsel ribbon, a rushing, shimmering blue turning to gold, to light, to heat – to blinding sunshine. Sand flew stinging past their faces as the bed skidded; then bumped; then stopped. They had arrived.

arey's first thought was that she wished she had
brought her hat. The white sand flung back the
dazzling glare of the sunlight in such a way that she
had to screw up her eyes to see.

The bed had done its best for them. It had set them down
on the very tip of a horse-shoe shaped reef. They found
themselves on a thin strip of fine white sand held in place by
walls of pitted coral. It was almost like being on a ship. In
the distance, across a lagoon of dazzling blue sea, they could
see the other tip of the horse-shoe. In between, a mile or so
away, where the front of the horse-shoe might be, were trees
and low hills.

In among the rocks, which formed the coral walls of their
narrow strip of land, were clear pools in which glimmered
seaweed of lovely colours, sea anemones, and transparent
fish. And the sand was as smooth and fine and white as icing
sugar. They had never seen sand like it. There were four
great scrapes in it where the bed had come to rest, but

beyond that not a footmark, not a ripple.

Charles kicked off his bedroom slippers and let his bare feet sink into the warm crust. It spurted up between his toes. 'Gosh,' he said happily.

Carey peered over at the lagoon. It was deep and clear. They could see strange fish swimming through the sunlit water. 'How lovely!' exclaimed Carey. 'How wonderful! Do let's go and explore.' Out at sea, between the two points of the horse-shoe, great waves rolled up and broke into swirls of spray, spreading their foam into the smooth surface of the lagoon.

Miss Price was unpacking. She took four bottles of ginger-pop out of the string bag and placed them in a pool to keep cool. The rest of the food, the hard-boiled eggs and the sandwiches, she put under the bed in the shade.

'You two big ones can explore,' she announced, 'but I'm going to sit here in the sun.' She retrieved her umbrella, her book, and the broomstick. Then sitting down on the sand, with her back against the bed, she methodically removed her shoes and stockings. Miss Price's feet, Carey noticed, were as pink and knobbly as her hands.

'Can we bathe?' asked Charles.

Miss Price adjusted her sun helmet and put up the umbrella. 'If you've brought your bathing-suits,' she said amiably, opening her book.

'We haven't. We didn't think of it.'

'Then why ask?' said Miss Price.

Charles and Carey looked at each other. Both had the same thought but neither spoke.

'You can paddle,' went on Miss Price, relenting a little. 'And explore. I'll take care of Paul.'

Paul, on the bed, was leaning over Miss Price's shoulder examining her book. 'Chapter Six,' he read aloud slowly. 'Another Man's Wife.' Miss Price shut the book on her finger.

'And you, Paul,' she said rather sharply, 'can take your bucket and spade and build sand castles.'

'I'd like to explore,' said Paul.

'No, you stay here and play by me. Jump down, and I'll roll up your pyjama legs.'

In the end it was agreed that Carey and Charles should go off by themselves, each with a bottle of ginger-pop, a hard-boiled egg, and a sandwich, and that they should all meet by the bed at about an hour before sunset. 'And don't be late.' Miss Price warned them. 'There's no twilight on these islands.'

Carey and Charles raced down the strip of sand towards the mainland. On one side of them lay the still lagoon, on the other the breakers broke on the coral rocks, and as they ran the children breathed the heady smell of spray. A faint breeze ran up their pyjama legs and down their sleeves, an airy coolness on their skin.

'Isn't this gorgeous?' cried Carey, increasing her speed.

'I'll say!' Charles shouted back.

The main beach, when they reached it, was fascinating. They found queer things among the flotsam and jetsam – bits of old spars, a bottle, sharks' eggs. The trees came down almost to the water's edge. A huge turtle scuttled by them into the sea, almost before they realized what it was. There were land crabs among the stones. Under the trees, as they went inland, the ground was smooth, a mixture of earth and sand. They found fallen coconuts and broke them on stones. They nearly went wild with delight when they found their first bread-fruit tree. They had read so much about bread-fruit.

'I don't think it's a bit like bread,' said Charles as he tasted it. 'It's more like spongy custard.'

They found a freshwater stream and following it up, through the rocks and creepers, they came to a silent pool. It was a lovely pool, where the roots of trees writhed down into the clear water, and in the middle of it was a smooth and sunlit rock. 'For diving,' said Charles. They were hot and tired, so, in spite of Miss Price, they threw off their pyjamas and bathed.

Once in the water, it was almost impossible to leave it. They dived and swam and sun-bathed. They ate their sandwiches and drank their ginger-pop. It tasted odd after so much coconut milk. Carey's plaits had come undone and her wet hair streaked about her like a mermaid's. They dozed a bit on the rock and talked and then they swam again.

'This can be our place for always,' said Carey. 'Our secret island. I never want to go anywhere else.'

There was no hurry to explore it all. They could come back again and again. They could build a house here, bring books, bring cooking things . . .

When at last they dressed, the sun was lower in the sky and the shadows had crept across the pool. Only in one corner gleamed a patch of golden light. They felt tired as they made their way once more towards the beach, climbing from rock to rock along the bed of the stream. Strange birds flew in and out among the dimness of the trees, and once they heard a hollow, almost human call. Carey shivered a little in her thin pyjamas. Her skin tingled from the sun and water, and her legs felt scratched.

When they came out of the shadows of the trees, the beach was no longer white but warm gold in the deep glow of the setting sun.

'I think we're a bit late,' said Carey. They shaded their eyes with their hands and looked across the lagoon towards the place where they had left the bed. 'There it is,' said Carey, almost with relief. 'But I don't see –' she hesitated. 'Can you see Miss Price and Paul?'

Charles strained his eyes. 'No. Not unless they're tucked up in bed,' he added.

'Then they did go exploring after all,' said Carey. 'We're back first anyway, even if we are late. Come on.'

'Wait a minute,' said Charles. He was staring across the lagoon. His face looked odd and blank.

'I say, Carey –'

'What?'

'The water's come up over that bar of sand.'

'What?' said Carey again. She followed the direction of his eyes. Smooth rollers were pouring over what had been their path, the spit of sand and coral along which they had raced so gaily that morning; smooth, combed-looking rollers, that poured into the smoothness of the lagoon, breaking a little where the coral ridge had held the sand. The bed, black against the glittering sea, stood as they had left it on a rising slope – an island, cut off.

Carey's face, in that golden light, looked expressionless and strange. They were silent, staring out across the water.

'Could you swim the lagoon?' asked Charles, after a moment. Carey swallowed. 'I don't know,' she said huskily.

'We might try it,' Charles suggested, rather uncertainly.

'What about Paul and Miss Price?' Carey reminded him.

'They may be tucked up in bed.' Charles screwed up his eyes. 'It's impossible to see, from here.'

'You'd see a lump or something. The outline of the bed looks too thin. Oh dear, Charles,' Carey burst out unhappily, 'it'll be dark soon.'

'Carey!' cried Charles suddenly.

She wheeled round, frightened by the note in his voice. He was looking up the beach towards the shadow of the trees. Three figures stood there, silent, and none of them was Miss Price or Paul; three dark figures, so still that at first Carey thought they could not be human. Then she shrieked – 'Cannibals!' she cried, and ran towards the sea. She did not stop to see if Charles was following her, she ran without thinking, without hearing, and almost without seeing, as a rabbit runs from the hunter or the cook from a mouse.

They caught her at the water's edge. She felt their breath on the back of her neck and then they gripped her by the arms. She screamed and kicked and bit and wriggled. There was nothing ladylike about Carey for quite five minutes. Then, all at once, she gave in. Sobbing and panting, she let them carry her up the beach, head downwards. In spite of her terror, she tried to look around for Charles. They had got him too, in the same position. 'Charles! Charles!' she cried. He did not, or could not, reply.

The man who had caught her made for the woods, and at each stride he took, her head bumped dizzily against his spine. He smelt of coconut oil and wore a belt of threaded teeth which, after a while, she took hold of to steady herself a little as she hung down his back. She could see the legs of Charles's captor and glimpses of the third man who ran along beside them. It was very dark in the woods, and, after a while, she heard the faint sound of drums. Of one thing we may be certain, Carey thought very little of the man who had described the island as being uninhabited. 'People should be careful,' she almost sobbed, pressing her face against the oily back to keep it out of the way of scratchy creepers, 'what they write in encyclopaedias.'

'Charles!' she called once when it had grown too dark to see.

'I'm here,' he shouted back in a panting, suffocated voice.

After a while, as the throb of the drums grew closer, she heard another sound, the chant of human voices: 'Ay oh . . . ay oh . . . ay . . . oh . . .' Then she saw a gleam of light. It shone on the boles of trees and the fronds of creepers. It became stronger and brighter until, at last, they found themselves in an open, firelit space where shadows moved and danced, and the earth vibrated to their dancing. 'Ay . . . oh . . . ay . . . oh . . . ay . . . oh,' went the voices.

It seemed to Carey, from what she could see in her upside-down position, that they had broken through the ring of dancers, because the firelight shone straight in her eyes and the voices, without changing their tune, swelled to a shout of pleased surprise – 'Ay . . . oh . . . ay . . . oh.'

Bump. Her captor let her drop on her head, as if she were a sack of potatoes. Dizzily she rolled into a sitting position and looked around for Charles. He crawled up to her. His forehead was bleeding, and he looked quite stunned.

Suddenly something pulled her hair. She jumped as if a snake had bitten her. She turned – and there was Paul. He looked very dirty – she could see that even by firelight – but he was smiling and saying something that she couldn't hear because of the noise of drums and voices.

'Paul!' she cried, and suddenly she felt less frightened. 'Where's Miss Price?'

Paul pointed – it was the easiest way. There sat poor Miss Price in the very middle of the circle. She was trussed up like a chicken, tied hand and foot with creepers. She still wore her sun helmet and a pair of dark glasses which glinted in the firelight.

Paul was shouting something in Carey's ear. She leaned closer.

'They're going to eat us,' Paul was saying. 'They've got the pot back there. They're cannibals.'

Carey marvelled at Paul's cheerfulness. 'Perhaps he imagines it's a dream,' she thought, wonderingly.

The dance began to quicken. The writhing bodies twisted and swayed. The voices became babbling so that the 'Ay . . . oh . . . ay . . . oh' became one word, and the drums increased their speed to a single humming note. There was a sudden shout. Then the dance stopped. There was a shuffling of feet; then silence.

Paul crept up between Charles and Carey. Carey took his hand.

The dancers stood quite still, like statues. They all looked inwards towards the children. Carey never knew what made her do it, but after a moment's hesitation, she let go Paul's hand and began to clap. Charles followed suit, and Paul joined in, enthusiastically, as if he were at the theatre.

The dancers smiled and looked quite shy. Then there was a mumble of unintelligible conversation, and everybody sat down cross-legged, like boy scouts round a camp fire. Miss Price was in the middle of the circle and nearest to the fire. The three children were grouped together, a little to one side.

After a moment there was a rattle of drums. The circle of eyes turned expectantly towards a path that wound between

the trees. Then there was a weird inhuman shout and a curious figure whirled into the firelight. If it had a face, you couldn't see it for paint. Daubs of scarlet and white hid the features. A great tail of shimmering feathers was attached to his belt at the back, and, as he whirled about, it shook as if he wagged it. He wore anklets of monkey's fur, and in one hand he carried a shinbone and in the other – of all things – Miss Price's broomstick!

'It's the witch-doctor,' said Charles in Carey's ear. Carey shivered. Looking round at the seated dancers, it seemed as if they had all drawn into themselves, as if they, too, were afraid. The weird object, his legs apart and knees bent, came jumping towards Miss Price. Every jump or so, he would whirl completely round. Each time he shook his feathers Paul laughed.

'Be quiet, Paul,' Carey urged him. 'You'll make him angry'; and Paul put his hand over his mouth, but he laughed just the same.

At last the witch-doctor stopped, just in front of Miss Price. He threw back his head and made a weird howl, a howl which seemed to echo across the island. Miss Price looked back at him through her dark glasses. The children could not see her expression.

Suddenly after a moment, there was another howl, higher, weirder, more piercing. The witch-doctor lowered the broomstick. There was something about his attitude which seemed bewildered.

Suddenly Carey laughed. She gripped her hands together. 'Charles,' she whispered excitedly, 'Miss Price did it. She did that last one.'

The witch-doctor recovered from his surprise. He gave two jumps in the air and then he howled again. It was a howl to end all howls. It went on and on. Carey imagined it echoing out across the reef, across the lagoon, across the darkening sea. Then the witch-doctor stopped. He stared at Miss Price. He seemed to be saying, 'Beat that, if you can.'

Miss Price moistened her lips. She wriggled her shoulders as if her bonds constrained her. Then she pursed up her mouth.

This time it was a whistle — a whistle so agonizingly piercing that it hurt one to hear it. It was like a steam engine in anguish, a needle-point of aching shrillness. The audience began to move, Carey gasped, and the witch-doctor clapped his hands to his ears and hopped round as if he were in pain.

When it stopped there was a murmur among the dancers. The witch-doctor swung round. He glared at them angrily.

'Hrrmph!' he grunted, and approached Miss Price once more.

She looked back at him impassively. The dark glasses were a great help. Carey crossed her thumbs. She remembered all Miss Price had said in the garden, about how few spells she knew by heart, how everything went out of her head if she were fussed, how you had to have something to turn into something and something to turn it *with*. 'Oh, Miss Price!' she breathed, 'Miss Price!' As people call the name of their side at a football match.

The witch-doctor held up the broomstick; with a twist he flung it into the air. It circled up into the darkness and came down turning slowly. He caught it with his other hand without looking at it.

There was a murmur of approbation among the crowd. They thought that was clever. The witch-doctor did a few satisfied jumps.

Miss Price laughed. ('Good,' thought Carey, 'she isn't fussed.')

The witch-doctor glared at her. She sat quite still; curiously still, thought Carey – but something was happening. The children stared hard. There was a space between Miss Price and the ground – a space which grew. Miss Price, still in a sitting position, had risen three feet in the air.

There was a murmur of amazement. Miss Price held her position. Carey could see her teeth were clenched and her face had become red. 'Go it, Miss Price,' she murmured. 'Hold it.' She gripped Charles's arm. Miss Price came down, plonk, rather suddenly. From her pained expression Carey guessed she had bitten her tongue, but the shock had broken the creepers which bound her hands. Miss Price put her fingers in her mouth as if to feel if her tongue were still there, then she rubbed her wrists, and glanced sideways at the children.

The witch-doctor did a few wild turns round the circle. He leaped into the air. He shouted, he twirled the broomstick. Carey noticed that every time he came too near the audience they shrank back a little. When he felt the onlookers were sufficiently subdued and suitably impressed, he stopped his caperings and flung Miss Price's broomstick away from him. He then sat down on his heels and stared at the broomstick. Nothing seemed to happen. The man was still. And so was the broomstick. But there was a waiting feeling in the air, something that prevented Carey from turning her eyes away towards Miss Price.

'Look,' said Charles suddenly. There was a gasp among the spectators, an amazed murmur. The broomstick was moving, in little jerks as if pulled by a string, towards the witch-doctor.

'Goodness!' said Charles. A funny feeling was creeping down his spine. This stirred him more than anything Miss Price had done. Miss Price, too, leaned forward. She pushed her dark glasses up on her forehead. Carey could see her expression. It was the face of one who was deeply and absorbedly interested. Steadily the broomstick moved on towards the witch-doctor, who sat as still as a statue made of stone. Silently he seemed to be calling it. If there had been pins on the island you could have heard one drop.

Miss Price stared a little longer at the broomstick and then she pulled her glasses down over her eyes again and bent her head. She looked almost as though she had fallen into a doze. The broomstick stopped within a few feet of the witch-doctor. It moved no further.

After a moment, the witch-doctor raised his head. He

looked round the circle and then he looked back again at Miss Price. She still sat with head sunk forward on her chest. The witch-doctor edged himself forward, on his behind, a little closer to the broomstick. 'Cheating,' whispered Carey furiously.

The broomstick again began to move, but this time it moved away from the witch-doctor; not in little jerks, but steadily, surely, it slid towards Miss Price. The witch-doctor hurriedly resumed his old position. The broomstick stopped.

'Oh dear,' exclaimed Carey. 'I can't bear it!'

Then reluctantly, in jerks, it began to move once more towards the witch-doctor. Miss Price bent her head still lower and clenched her hands. Carey could see her knuckles shining in the firelight. The broomstick hesitated, then, with a rush, it slid across the sandy ground straight into Miss Price's lap. She gripped it firmly. She threw up her head. The witch-doctor leapt to his feet. He gave three jumps, one awful howl, and moved towards Miss Price; in his hand gleamed something long and sharp. Gripping the broomstick, Miss Price faced him sternly. Her feet were tied, she could not move.

Carey cried out and hid her eyes, but Paul, sitting up on his heels, shouted excitedly: 'A frog! A yellow frog! Miss Price! You did that lying down!'

Miss Price glanced at Paul, a sideways thankful look. She gasped. Then she held out her two arms toward the witch-doctor as if to ward him off with the broomstick. He stopped, with knees bent, about to jump. Then he seemed to shrink and dwindle. He sank downwards into his legs as if the heat of the fire was melting him. The children held their breaths as they watched. Every part of him was shrinking at

the same time. It reminded Carey of what happened to a
lead soldier when you threw it on the fire, but instead of a
blob of silver, the witch-doctor melted into a minute blob of
gold, a tiny yellowish object, barely distinguishable upon
the sandy ground.

'You see!' screamed Paul. 'She did it! She couldn't do it
quickly, but she did it!'

Carey leaned forward, trying to see better. Suddenly the
blob jumped. Carey shrieked. Paul laughed. He was very
excited. 'It's only a frog,' he crowed, 'a tuppenny-ha'penny
little frog . . . a silly old frog.' Carey slapped him.

'Be quiet,' she hissed. 'We're not safe yet.'

There was a strange silence among the dancers. They
seemed afraid – afraid of the frog, afraid of Miss Price, afraid
even of the children.

'Carey!' called Miss Price. She was untying the creepers
which bound her feet. Carey ran to her. Charles and Paul
followed.

'You'll all have to hold on to the broomstick. It will be
hard but it won't be for long. We must get to the bed. When I
shriek, you must all shriek and that will help the broomstick
to rise.'

'Four people on a broomstick,' gasped Carey.

'I know. It's dangerous but it's our only hope. Paul can
come on my knee, but you and Charles must just hang on.
Now don't forget: when I shriek, you all shriek.'

Miss Price took Paul on her knee. She gripped the tip of
the broomstick with both hands. Carey and Paul took hold
of the wood. Miss Price shut her eyes a moment as if she were
trying to recall the spell. The frog had disappeared, but the
dancers, watching them suspiciously, suddenly began to
move forward. Hurriedly Miss Price gabbled her verse:

'Frog's spawn; toad's eye.
Newts swim, bats FLY . . .'

As she said 'FLY' her voice rose to a resounding shriek. The children joined in. The broomstick rose a little off the ground. Carey and Charles were hanging by their hands.

'Bats FLY – Y – Y,' shrieked Miss Price again as a hint to the broomstick. It made a valiant effort. It wobbled slowly upward. The natives ran forward. Knives flashed, but Carey and Charles were just out of reach, dangling. Then Carey saw a man was fitting an arrow to a bow.

'FLY – Y – Y,' shrieked Miss Price again.

'For goodness' sake!' added Charles. His pyjama trousers were slipping off. He felt very vulnerable.

Whether or not this unexpected addition to the spell acted as a spur it is hard to say, but the broomstick gave a sudden leap forwards and upwards.

The circle of firelight and the gesticulating dancers dropped away below them, and they were above the moonlit trees and there ahead lay the glimmer of the sea. The broomstick swayed and plunged but kept its course, making for the point of the reef. Carey and Charles hung on for dear life. Their arms felt numb and almost pulled from their sockets and a cold wind whistled through their night clothes.

Above the lagoon, the broomstick swerved; sickeningly it began to circle downwards. Carey and Charles floated up sideways as the broomstick dived. Carey strained her eyes. She could only see breakers, breakers and spray and moonlit waters. Was the bed submerged? 'Oh,' she cried, as the broomstick gathered speed, making straight for the waves. Then suddenly she saw the bed. It was not yet under water.

It stood just where they had left it on the rising strip of sand. But as they landed she saw a great wave swell up, gather height, and curl.

'Wish, Paul, wish,' shrieked Carey madly. Then the wave broke over them. Gasping, spluttering, soaked to the skin, they clung to the slippery bed rails.

Paul must have wished. The bed rolled and lurched, then spun into space. The darkness thinned as they whistled through it. A pale light grew around them, deepening to gold, and rose and blue and yellow – flowers, twisted into nosegays and tied with blue ribbon . . . Carey stared, and then she recognized the pattern. It was the early sunlight shining on Paul's wall-paper . . .

They were home, but what a mess! All their pyjamas were ragged and dirty, their dressing-gowns lost, and the bed was soaked. Poor Miss Price was a sorry sight. Her sun helmet was soft and soggy. She had no shoes or stockings and her coat and skirt dripped puddles on the floor. Of her belongings, all she had left was the broomstick. Haggardly, she peered out of the window.

'It's too light to fly,' she muttered. Then an awful thought seemed to strike her. 'It must be after nine o'clock.' She sat down limply on a chair. As she sat, she squelched. 'Goodness me, Carey, here's a nice to-do!'

Charles went to the window. It was open, just as they had left it.

'There's no one about,' he said. 'Just use the broomstick as far as the ground and then make a run for it.'

Miss Price stared at him blankly. 'Oh dear,' she exclaimed, 'this is terrible.'

'Yes, Miss Price, you must,' urged Carey. 'Make a run for it.'

Miss Price looked at her naked bony feet. 'If I should meet the gardener . . .' she pointed out helplessly.

'You must risk it,' said Carey.

'Listen!' whispered Charles, raising his head.

Yes. Unmistakably there were footsteps coming upstairs.

'Quick, Miss Price.' Carey pushed the broomstick into Miss Price's unwilling hand. They helped her over the sill

'Oh dear,' Miss Price muttered to herself as gingerly she clung to the coping. 'This is not the way to do things.'

'I know,' whispered Carey, giving Miss Price a little shove, 'but it can't be helped.'

They watched Miss Price float slowly down, then they watched her pick up her skirts and the broomstick and make for the shelter of the bushes. They drew a sharp breath of relief as she reached cover and then they turned – to face the eyes of Elizabeth.

'Breakfast,' said Elizabeth, standing in the doorway, 'has been on the table this half-hour –' She paused. Then her mouth fell open. She was staring at the floor. Carey, looking downwards, saw a large black puddle spreading slowly from the bed towards Elizabeth's feet. Elizabeth's eyes followed the stream to its source. Her mouth opened wider and her gaze travelled slowly from the bed to the children. It took in their appearance from top to toe, the smudged faces, the wet hair, the peeling noses, the torn pyjamas clinging limply, to the sun-scorched limbs.

'Well –' said Elizabeth slowly, 'I never!' Then she shut her mouth with a snap. Her eyes glared. Colour mounted slowly to her pallid cheeks. 'This,' said Elizabeth, 'is the end.'

Deliberately she looked round once more. She picked up a corner of the eiderdown. It was dark red instead of pale pink. It hung heavily between her thumb and forefinger. Regular clock-like drips drummed gently on the polished floor. She let it fall. She stared at it a moment unbelievingly and then once more she looked at Paul and Carey. She smiled, a grim, menacing little smile which did not reach her eyes. 'All right,' she said calmly and, turning, left the room.

The three children stood quiet. In silence and misery they stood while the puddles deepened round their feet, and the drips from the eiderdown ticked off the heavy seconds. At last Carey moved. She pushed back her wet hair.

'Come, Paul,' she said huskily. 'Let's go to the bathroom and wash.'

'What I don't understand,' said Aunt Beatrice for the fourth time, 'is from where you got the water. The bathroom's right down the passage, and there isn't a jug.'

The children gazed back at her. They were in the study. Aunt Beatrice sat at her desk turning a little sideways so that she could face them as they stood in a row on the carpet. There was a closed look in their faces, though their eyes were round and candid. '*Whatever happens*,' Carey had warned them, 'we mustn't give away Miss Price. Except for that it doesn't matter what we say because nothing could be worse.'

Carey cleared her throat. She did not reply, but stood staring unwaveringly at her aunt's face.

'The charitable attitude to adopt, Carey,' said Aunt Beatrice in her precise, cutting voice, 'is that you are not quite right in your head. This story about a South Sea island, cannibals . . . lagoons. . . . If it were necessary to lie, a child of three could do better.'

Carey swallowed.

'A magic bed . . .' Aunt Beatrice smiled acidly. 'It might interest you to know, Carey, that I bought that bed myself in 1903, quite new, from Baring & Willow's – a most reputable firm,' she added, 'and not given to innovations.'

Carey changed her weight from her left foot to her right.

'What I still don't understand,' reiterated Aunt Beatrice, 'is from where you got the water.'

'From the sea,' said Paul suddenly. 'Carey told you.'

Aunt Beatrice raised her almost hairless eyebrows. She picked up her pen and turned back to her desk. Her thin smile was far from reassuring.

'No matter,' she said. 'I have wired your mother, and Elizabeth is packing your things – the last service Elizabeth will perform for me. After all these years she has given me notice.'

'But it's true, Aunt Beatrice,' Carey burst out. 'It was the sea. You can prove it.'

Aunt Beatrice half turned, the pen delicately suspended in her birdlike hand.

'How, may I ask?' she inquired ironically.

'By licking the blanket, Aunt Beatrice,' said Carey politely.

Aunt Beatrice's pink-rimmed eyes became like agates.

'You are not my children,' she said coldly, 'and I am not as young as I was; there is no reason at all why I should put up with this sort of thing! Your mother, job or no job, must make other arrangements for you. I have finished. You may go.'

They crept to the door. At the threshold they paused; Aunt Beatrice was speaking again. 'As there are no taxis,' she was saying, 'Mr Bisselthwaite, the milkman, has very kindly consented to pick you up at 11.45 at the end of the lane. Your train leaves at twelve.'

Gently, gently they closed the door.

FAREWELL

The milkman was late. 'Perhaps,' said Carey, as they stood in the grass by the side of the lane, 'we could just run in and say goodbye to Miss Price.'

'One of us had better stay,' said Charles, 'to look after the bags and wait for the milk-cart. You and Paul go.'

Carey hesitated. 'All right,' she said, after a moment. 'And you can come along in the cart.'

Miss Price was in her front garden. When she saw Carey and Paul in coats and hats she looked surprised. She set down her wheelbarrow and waited between the shafts. Carey ran up to her.

'Miss Price,' she said, 'we're going.'

'Going where?' asked Miss Price. Her face looked tired and rather pale except for the sunburn on the long thin nose.

'Home. To London.'

'Oh dear,' said Miss Price. She looked distressed. She began to pull off her gardening gloves.

'It was the bed and the water and everything. We're being

sent away. But we did keep our promise, Miss Price. We never told about you.'

'Oh dear,' said Miss Price again. She sat down on the edge of the wheelbarrow.

Paul, very subdued, began to collect dead flower heads from the rubbish.

'We came to say goodbye,' went on Carey.

'Oh dear,' said Miss Price for the third time. 'I feel very much to blame. We shouldn't have gone to that island, but,' she went on, 'I thought a nice quiet day, a breath of sea air . . .' She paused.

'Look,' Paul broke in. 'A pink cabbage.'

Carey looked down. There it lay among the rubbish, Miss Price's giant rosebud!

'Oh, Miss Price –' exclaimed Carey, staring at it. It must have weighed a couple of pounds.

Miss Price coloured. 'I have done a lot of thinking since yesterday, Carey. I've been thinking about last night and what you said about the flower show –' She glanced at Paul as if to include him in her observations. 'I've been thinking that magic may be a kind of cheating. It looks good to start with, but perhaps it doesn't bring good results in the end.'

Paul frowned. 'I've had wonderful results from cheating,' he said stubbornly.

'I don't suppose I'll give it up altogether,' went on Miss Price, ignoring Paul and holding on to her gentle smile. 'But I thought I'd try to give it up for a while.'

They were all silent. 'Oh, Miss Price,' murmured Carey rather sadly. She shared Paul's disappointment.

'It gets such a hold on one,' said Miss Price.

There was an awful pause. Paul had turned back the leaves of the pink cabbage. A sweet dry smell of sun-warmed deadness rose from the barrow.

'I have decided,' went on Miss Price, watching Paul's fingers, 'in future to regard witchcraft – not as a hobby,' she paused, 'but as a weakness.'

'Darling Miss Price,' cried Carey suddenly, 'you're such a good sport.' She flung her arms round Miss Price's neck. She felt the wetness of a tear on Miss Price's long nose. 'Thank you, Miss Price, for everything, even the cannibals.'

It was a moving moment. Paul looked glumly, a little bewildered. He had an uneasy feeling that Miss Price was turning over a new leaf before he had finished with the old one. It was almost a relief when the milk-cart rattled up to the gate. Miss Price wiped her eyes.

'Now you must go,' she said, straightening her hat as Charles jumped down off the milk-cart to shake her hand. She tried to smile. 'Good luck, dear children, and goodbye. Keep your warm hearts, your gentleness, and your courage. These will do,' said Miss Price, sniffing audibly, 'just as well as magic.'

She turned away hurriedly; squaring her shoulders, she picked up the handles of the wheelbarrow and trundled it off towards the rubbish heap.

The milkman cracked his whip and they clattered away amid the cheerful jangle of empty cans.

'She won't keep it up,' said Paul, who, unobserved, had edged himself into the place nearest the pony.

In the train, Charles frowned through the window. Carey had told him of the conversation with Miss Price.

'Magic may be just a weakness,' he said, 'but it's better than some weaknesses.'

'I know,' agreed Carey.

'If we still had the bed, I think I'd use it,' Charles went on. 'Sometimes.'

'Yes,' said Carey. 'Just sometimes.'

'The bed wasn't magic,' put in Paul consolingly. 'It was only the bed-knob that was magic.'

'Well, it's the same thing,' said Carey, turning irritably from Paul, who, kneeling up on his seat, was breathing in her face. 'One thing's no good without the other.'

'Couldn't you use a magic bed-knob on another bed the same make?'

'Oh, I don't know, Paul.' Carey edged away from him, closer to the window. 'What's the good of talking about it if we haven't got either. Do sit down properly!'

Paul meekly put his legs down, so that they dangled just above the floor. He leaned back, sucking his cheeks in. One hand was in his pocket, fidgeting. He looked worried. 'But,' he protested, after some moments of silent thought, 'I did bring the bed-knob.'